For grandpa bears everywhere
~ A.R.

For Andi—a wonderful grandpa and treasured friend
~ A.E.

tiger tales
5 River Road, Suite 128, Wilton, CT 06897
Published in the United States 2019
Originally published in Great Britain 2019
by Little Tiger Press Ltd.
Text copyright © 2019 Alison Ritchie
Illustrations copyright © 2019 Alison Edgson
ISBN-13: 978-1-68010-131-7
ISBN-10: 1-68010-131-5
Printed in China
LTP/1400/2466/1018
All rights reserved
10 9 8 7 6 5 4 3 2 1

For more insight and activities, visit us at www.tigertalesbooks.com

Me and My Grandpa!

by Alison Ritchie • *Illustrated by* Alison Edgson

 tiger tales

My grandpa is here.
It's the BEST kind of day!
I hop on his back,
and we're off on our way.

As we skip through the woods,
there's SO much to see.
We call out the names
of each flower and tree.

We slide down the hillside
and land with a thud.
Grandpa looks funny
all covered in mud!

It's time to clean up,
so we jump in the lake.
Grandpa's BIG splash
makes the whole forest shake!

When we play hide-and-seek,
I climb right up the tree.
Grandpa is clever,
but he never finds me!

With his bright, beaming smile
and a cheery hello,
My grandpa makes friends
wherever we go!

While Grandpa picks berries,
I carry the pot.
A few make it in—
but a whole bunch do not!

If something is wrong
and I start to feel blue,
My grandpa is there
and knows just what to do!

The fort we've been building
is finished at last.
I clamber inside it,
but Grandpa's stuck fast!

As the sun starts to set,
we sing songs by the fire.
Our friends join in, too—
we're the marshmallow choir!

When it's bedtime back home,
Grandpa tucks me in tight.
Then he gives me a hug
and a big kiss good night.

Grandpa's my hero—
he's funny and smart.
I love my grandpa
with ALL of my heart.